Bare Bear's
New Clothes

Written by Peter Seymour
Illustrated by Robert Cremins

Fuzzy Wuzzy was a Bear,
But Fuzzy Wuzzy lost his hair.
So Fuzzy Wuzzy's friends came by
And brought new clothes for him to try.

You can help, too.
Turn each page to put
a new outfit on Fuzzy.

Copyright © 1986 by Intervisual Communications, Inc.
Published by Price Stern Sloan, Inc., 360 North La Cienega Boulevard, Los Angeles, California 90048.

Fuzzy tried a clown suit on,
All spots and pink and frilly.
Fox and Rabbit both agreed
That Fuzzy looked too silly.

"This sailor suit," said Rabbit,
"We found floating in the sea."
"It must have shrunk!" cried Fuzzy,
"It's much too tight for me!"

"If you were a great magician,
You could pull me from your hat,"
Said Rabbit. "No! On second thought,
You're much too rough for that!"

Fuzzy tried on cowboy clothes,
But said, "I fear I lack
The skill for riding horses
On a saddle or bare back!"

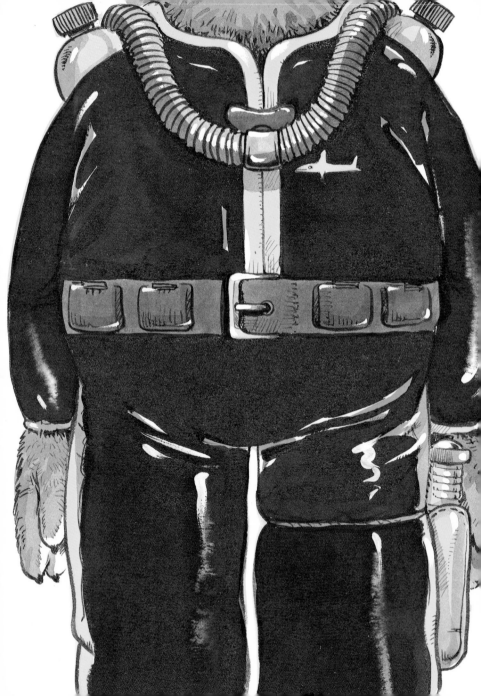

Rabbit brought a wet suit,
And Frog said, "Follow me!"
But Fuzzy said, "I'm frightened
Of what lurks in the sea!"

Fox brought out pajamas
But Fuzzy shook his head.
"Can't you see that Frog and I
Don't want to go to bed!"

"Be a drum major," said Fox,
"You look very grand."
But Rabbit groaned, "I can't stand
The noise of Fuzzy's band!"

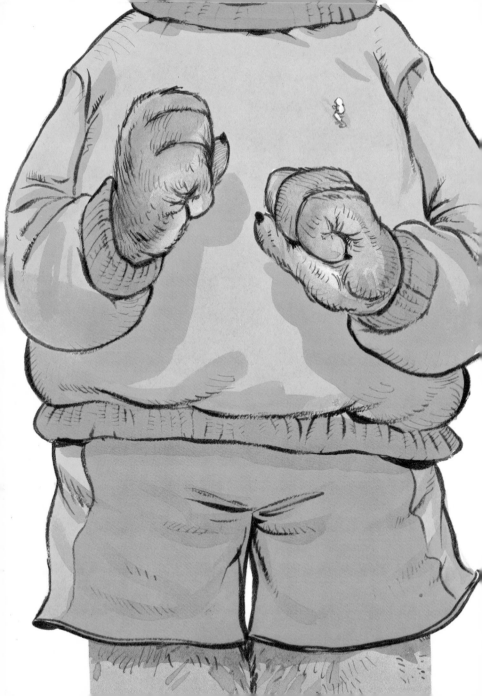

"You need a jogging outfit,"
Said Fox. "Come on, get going!"
But Rabbit said, "It's no good, Fuzz,
I fear your fat is showing!"

"An astronaut," said Rabbit,
"Can watch the world go round."
But Fuzzy said, "I much prefer
To keep my feet upon the ground!"